W9-ABV-416

This Year's Garden

This Year's Garden

by Cynthia Rylant • pictures by Mary Szilagyi

BRADBURY PRESS / SCARSDALE, NEW YORK

 Bradbury Press, Inc. 2 Overhill Road, Scarsdale, N.Y. An affiliate of Macmillan, Inc. Collier Macmillan Canada, Inc. Manufactured in the United States of America 10 9 8 7 6 5 4 3 2 1 The text of this book is set in 16 pt. Century Textbook. The illustrations are colored-pencil drawings, reproduced in full color.

Library of Congress Cataloging in Publication Data Rylant, Cynthia. This year's garden. Summary: Follows the seasons of the year as reflected in the growth, life, and death of the garden of a large rural family. 1. Children's stories, American. [1. Gardens — Fiction. 2. Seasons — Fiction] I. Szilagyi, Mary, ill. II. Title PZ7.R982Th 1984 [E] 84-10974
ISBN 0-02-777970-X

For Karen and Jennifer; Joe and Leeanne; Shannon, Kevin, and Jenny; and especially Megan and Nate
–C.R.

To Mary Ellen
–M.S.

At the end of winter, we all go down and stare a while. Uncle Dean squatting and chewing on a weed to think.

A garden after winter is a wonder to see. All brown stalks and black birds working. Quiet. Just brown and waiting for someone.

Uncle Dean and Uncle Joe discuss what we'll plant this year. Figuring on more potatoes but fewer beans because Granny said she's not canning an army's worth of beans this year. Granny's getting tired of canning.

We're all a little disappointed because we all like beans.

We stare at the garden a while longer, feeling Spring on us and ready to run for a hoe.

But first we have to wait. For the rain to stop. For the ground to dry up and the weather to warm up. Waiting for the last frost.

And finally, close to June, we are planting. All of us bending, dropping seeds as we walk backwards while someone follows with a hoe. Wide straw hats bobbing in the garden.

We are quiet in the heat, talkative when it gets cool. Talking about picking some poke for salad and will the tomatoes blight and what about some eggplant this year?

We look a lot alike, too. Noses and arms up to the sleeves sunburned. Purely white foreheads, those of us with hats. And fingernails just full of dirt.

Then, later in the summer, we have a garden. Full of vegetables and mole holes. Beetles and big grass spiders. Late in the evening the beagles run through, crying after a rabbit or maybe a possum.

We hurry down to pull some carrots for company.
Or turn over potatoes to wheel into the cellar.

Shucking corn. Snapping beans. Stewing tomatoes. And canning lids popping so much we think we hear them in our sleep.

And when the vines and stalks are empty, when the soil's all been turned, and it is blowing into Winter, we sit with the neighbors and compare. About who had the best luck with this year's garden.

Outside, the garden's brown again. The crows are back. And we are, all of us, waiting . . . for next year's garden.